1,000,000 Books
are available to read at

Forgotten Books

www.ForgottenBooks.com

Read online
Download PDF
Purchase in print

ISBN 978-0-259-55038-9
PIBN 10822926

This book is a reproduction of an important historical work. Forgotten Books uses state-of-the-art technology to digitally reconstruct the work, preserving the original format whilst repairing imperfections present in the aged copy. In rare cases, an imperfection in the original, such as a blemish or missing page, may be replicated in our edition. We do, however, repair the vast majority of imperfections successfully; any imperfections that remain are intentionally left to preserve the state of such historical works.

Forgotten Books is a registered trademark of FB &c Ltd.
Copyright © 2018 FB &c Ltd.
FB &c Ltd, Dalton House, 60 Windsor Avenue, London, SW19 2RR.
Company number 08720141. Registered in England and Wales.

For support please visit www.forgottenbooks.com

1 MONTH OF FREE READING

at

www.ForgottenBooks.com

By purchasing this book you are eligible for one month membership to ForgottenBooks.com, giving you unlimited access to our entire collection of over 1,000,000 titles via our web site and mobile apps.

To claim your free month visit:
www.forgottenbooks.com/free822926

* Offer is valid for 45 days from date of purchase. Terms and conditions apply.

English
Français
Deutsche
Italiano
Español
Português

www.forgottenbooks.com

Mythology Photography **Fiction** Fishing Christianity **Art** Cooking Essays Buddhism Freemasonry Medicine **Biology** Music **Ancient Egypt** Evolution Carpentry Physics Dance Geology **Mathematics** Fitness Shakespeare **Folklore** Yoga Marketing **Confidence** Immortality Biographies Poetry **Psychology** Witchcraft Electronics Chemistry History **Law** Accounting **Philosophy** Anthropology Alchemy Drama Quantum Mechanics Atheism Sexual Health **Ancient History Entrepreneurship** Languages Sport Paleontology Needlework Islam **Metaphysics** Investment Archaeology Parenting Statistics Criminology **Motivational**

THE CHRISTMAS NUMBER OF THE "WASP" SUPPLEMENT INCLUSIVE, 10 CENTS ONLY!

Published every Saturday,
—AT—
602 CALIFORNIA ST., cor. Kearny.

LOUIS SOLSCHER, Business Manager.

TERMS·
CITY SUBSCRIBERS
THIRTY-FIVE CENTS PER MONTH delivered by carrier, Single copies, ten cents.

BY MAIL
To all parts of the United States, Canada and British Columbia,
(INVARIABLY IN ADVANCE)
(Postage Free)

One Year	$4.00
Six Months	$2.00
Three Months	$1.00

TO ALL PARTS OF EUROPE, AUSTRALIA, MEXICO, SOUTH AMERICA, SANDWICH ISLANDS, Etc. Etc.
(Postage Free)

One Year	$5.0
Six Months	$2.0
Three Months	$1.25

TAKE NOTICE.
A TWO CENT STAMP mails the WASP anywhere. BACK NUMBERS of the WASP for sale at this office. All Postmasters are authorized to take subscriptions for the WASP, payable invariably in advance.

G. BOHNCKE and ED. PRATT. are the only authorized traveling agents for the WASP in California.

THURSDAY, DECEMBER 25, 1879.

SALMI MORSE, - - MANAGING EDITOR.

THE WASP has the felicity to wish you a MERRY CHRISTMAS ! and to present you with an acceptable issue to divert the time on memorable Christmas Day.

Our number to-day, is entirely from the beaten path. We have purposely chosen matter which is most adaptable to the occasion, and have intentionally conspired to waft the reader to other spheres, by means of our subjects chosen. Nearly everything is of a nature Oriental. "The Phantom Ship" is particularly worthy of note; it is a stereotyped tale of the Orient, and is told to nearly every tourist having a taste that way, and the author wonders at never having met with it in print, although it has always been his firm belief, that the ground work for Captain Marryat's "Flying Dutchman" has been taken from this tale.

The scene from a *Midwinter Night's Dream* and another from *Gustavus Adolphus*, are extracts from unpublished plays of the editor. Their fitness to the season we celebrate, having prompted him to adopt them for the occasion.

Our readers need not be reminded that everything the WASP holds forth, is at all times strictly original. ED. WASP.

THE LESSON OF THE SEASON.

A Merry Christmas to All!

Christmas is here again. It is a matter of small moment, except to the historian particular in dates, whether Our Saviour was born on the day we have chosen to celebrate the event, or not. It may be true that the anniversary of the Natal Day of Him, whom Isaiah foretold as the Wonderful, the Counsellor, the Prince of Peace, and on whose shoulder would be the government of the world, was formerly fixed in Midsummer, and that a certain Pope transferred the observance to midwinter, to suit the convenience of pilgrims in warm climates; and it may also be true, that the Eastern church hallowed the fourth of January in commemoration of this notable occasion. Kepler, Chrysostom, Eusebius, Sulpicius, and a score or more of ancient worthies, differ regarding the precise time the long promised Messiah came into this wicked world, and commenced that tremendous drama in which the Heavens and the earth, were deeply interested spectators. How can we, then, at this late day, and with less perfect means of information than the Fathers possessed, hope to arrive at the exact date? We do not propose to attempt it. We prefer to regard the nativity of our Lord and Saviour, Jesus Christ, simply from the stand point of the beneficial effects which its commemoration has on humanity.

We have our patriotic holiday to celebrate the birth of the nation; we have a day set apart on which to do honor to' the name of our glorious Washington; a day to thank the Almighty for the blessings of the year; but there is a marked difference in the effect of the observance of these times and seasons, compared with the influence of Christmas Day.

More or less of selfish feelings, enter into the observance of each anniversary named, excepting the day we are now celebrating.

We do not propose to write an essay on selfishness; but may lay down, as a general proposition, that this quality is now accepted as the basis of human character, the motor of human action. It seems, in fact, no matter how much we condemn selfishness in theory, that we are bound to accept it in practice, and to admit that it is necessary to modern social cohesion as well as to individual advancement. In the race of life, in the push for wealth and position, he only wins, who takes no thought but for himself, or, if for others, only in so far, as they may be useful to him in accomplishing selfish purposes. Such, we repeat, seems to be the necessity and the fashion of the time, which, while admitting, we regret. We trample on the weak while endeavoring to pull down the strong, and, if successful, are ourselves, in turn, pulled down by others still more powerful. And so the strife goes on. Ego is set up in the temples of Wealth and Ambition, as the principal idol, and crowds of worshipers prostrate themselves at its base. This strife would go on ceaselessly, until we became like the beasts in our selfish ferocity, were not certain days—such as the hallowed day of which we are writing —mercifully interposed to give, whatever there is in us of the higher nature, time for assertion; time, we may say, without being accused of flippancy for the soul to cleanse itself, in some degree, from the smirch of selfish worldliness. Unselfishness is the lesson of the season. When we hear, above the turmoil of our work-a-day life

* * "the bells on Christmas Day.
Their old familiar carols play,
And wild and sweet
The words repeat,
Of peace on earth, good will to men!"

there must come to every heart a feeling as unselfish as it is possible for poor sinning and suffering humanity to entertain—a feeling that disposes us to give good gifts to all who ask us, in the name of Him who gave his life to purify and redeem our souls at last. With the sound of the Christmas bells we rise out of Self, and get away, for the nonce, from the narrow considerations of class and country. We find ourselves elevated to a plane, where we could stand in common brotherhood with all mankind,

"And think how, as the day had come,
The belfries of all Christendom,
How rolled along,
The unbroken song,
Of peace on earth, good will to men."

Unselfishness is the lesson of the season, because Christ, from the manger to the cross, lived not for himself alone, but for others, and one of the good effects of Christmas is that we are apt to make a contrast of his character with that of our own and of human nature in general. When we mentally recount the incidents in his life, how utterly contemptible we become in our own estimation! How narrow our widest charities are in comparison with a philanthropy that embraced a world!—and what moral cowards we seem, when we think of his calm bravery that in the cause of Man's salvation, stood unabashed before the Princes and Powers of the Earth. In a healthy mind these considerations ought to impart a firmer tone to good purposes, and weaken if not wholly dismiss, the questionable and bad.

Unselfishness taught on Christmas Day could not be lasting. But lasting enough for us to find more Scrooges unlocking their money-hoards to relieve the distress that is around us on every hand, and to cause more Tiny Tim's, folding their hands in thoughtfulness, to say

"GOD BLESS US ALL !"

THE charm of human life is its charming humanity, It is a religion within a religion, as Christmas has its holidays within a holiday. The delight of the parents at the delights manifested by the children, because they are their parents; the delights consequent upon the exchange of friendly appreciation; the gratification upon the gratefulness of a grateful remembrance; the happiness which redounds from a happiness created upon others; the inherent excellencies which excel every other inherency in man; all these manifest themselves gratefully at Christmas time, and build an entirely independent little world, within the world so much dependent upon it. When we see the smiling family faces gathered around our board each contented, how can we be otherwise than content with all? Content that we are content, content that others are content, content that each is with one another content. This only happens at Christmas time, let us therefore glorify the hallowed time!

THE HAMMAM
OF
HAROUN AL RASHID
AT
BAGDAD.

The Hammam of Haroun al Rashid at Bagdad, has reputation throughout the globe, for its antiquity, and the great repute of its reputable founder. Although not the actual founder of the noted Caliphate, yet Haroun al Rashid (Aaron the Just) had the astute ability of centralizing it. His sagacity accomplished the organization of a powerful empire, from out a jumble of undefined possessions, an achievement which exercised no little influence in after time, upon the destinies of the entire human race.

To this day, all the past glories of this once most famous Hammam, have merged into one notable attribute, for which it still stands in significant prominence throughout the Orient—its incomparable story-tellers.

Story telling in the far Orient, is in many ways a profession; it performs the function, but in a verbal way, of the Murrays, Appletons, and Harpers of our portion of the world—a sort of scholarly verbal printing press and itinerant library for the diffusion of moral precepts and innocent delights. Their stories are stereotyped, but their particular embellishments are individual accomplishments. Agreeable to entertainments everywhere, there are among the fraternity, stock and star actors. Ibraim Melek, the Edmund Kean of the Euphrate region, a man of wonderful story-telling proficiency, stood at the head of his profession, and journeyed from Damascus to this place for a season.

They have their public and private seances. A foreigner is compelled to put on appearances, else he has a hard life of it in the Orient. The child of the desert loves dazzle, glitter and pomp; and if a foreigner has a desire to be entertained by an exalted personage like Ibraim Melek, he has to command an exclusive performance or lose cast.

Luxuriating over my coffee, sherbet, and chibuque, in commodious *dishabille*, upon a voluptuous ottoman, at the finish of the operations of the bath, I requested the renowned genius to my presence, and from a choice of *repertoire*, rendered by his familiar in attendance, in a verbal hand bill way, I selected that which follows:

"A company of travelling merchants," began Ibraim Melek, "were journeying from Damascus to Bagdad, Yakub Fedir Khan in their midst.

It was arranged from the start, that at each camping, the companions should, in turn, relate a notable phase of their individual life, with the privilege of the last speaker to call upon whomsoever his choice falls as next.

"Yakub Fedir Khan," exclaimed the last speaker, we are prepared to listen to a phase of your wonderful life. We, who have known your parentage, and have followed your father to the grave, an honorable but poor man. You are his son, still young, of great enterprise, to be sure, but wealthy beyond comparison. Tell us of your first start in life, and the manner of your having met with such unbounded success."

"Yes," put in Ibram Pacha "not a grain of sand glows in the desert sun, but your every camel has had his shadow upon it. Were the Caliphate for sale, you have the wealth to buy it. Tell us Yakub, we are burning to hear you."

Yakub Fedir Kahn, took a long whiff at his *nargilly*.

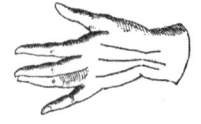

"My friends," he calmly said, elevating his one hand which was gloved, "*my fortune was made by the loss of my one hand!*"

"The loss of your one hand!" exclaimed all in a breath.

"Yes," said Yakub quietly, "you are all aware that my father's poverty was due to his ambition to have me excel, and my wealth is due to that which made him poor. He would have me educated as the Franks are, and sent me first to Paris, then to Leghorn, and lastly to Venice, where I had the good luck to lose the hand which made my fortune.

"Allah achbar!" again exclaimed his companions all in a breath.

"It is true, exclaimed Yakub Pedir Khan, and if you will lend me your patience, I'll give you the

HISTORY OF MY LOST HAND.

You see this hand; I open and shut it, I stroke my beard, guide the pen with it, and make it convene to my every desire, yet it is but a mechanical hand, a masterwork executed in London, and substitutes the hand and wrist, lopped off by the public executioner at Venice.

The function it performs so admirably, is owing to the fact of many straps passing over my shoulder, and around my body; these in their turn act upon springs inside the woodwork beneath this glove; any strain upon the straps, invests it with the functions of life, and I have not the slightest doubt, the time is not far distant when complete men will be constructed from both wood and metal, who by automatom labor on their part, will almost relieve mankind of the galling drudgeries of his daily active life.

For no discrepancy, nor for violation of any act, legal or divine, yet for a deed upon which I prefer to keep silent, I was chained down, to tinder up, under the singeing leads of the condemned cells of Venice.

To conceive the degree of torture a culprit is submitted to in the glowing den, is to figure a half-fed wretch designedly stinted of water and immured in a bake oven, of a suffocating atmosphere, which tindered, cindered and broiled by slow degrees.

Even were I not chained to the eternal stone wall, I could not have availed myself of the exercise the limited space held out, for the leaden roof was so low, that an outspread hand would have filled all the space between it, and the cropped head of the doomed. Everything I touched was glowing with heat, and the small supply of water, which I husbanded to make it last, in five minutes partook of the glow of the earthen jug, which burned like the intensified chain, like the lead covered floor, the lead casings of the wall, and last of all, the glowing, hot leads overhead. Suffocating is no word for the pernicious atmosphere, yet I managed to breathe. There was a constant battering of my brains and temples, yet I lived. An unremitting buffet welled my blood-flooded eyes, yet I slept. But rats and insects invaded the dreadful precincts from choice, and pestered me until my body festered to sores, which from constancy of annoyance, at last lost their quality to annoy, and of the many under the leads, I was sufferer as any, but no more.

By a hole in the wall, the height of the pitcher, a loaf of coarse brown bread, found its way to me each day. Not but there was a door, but this opened to State prisoners twice only; once when led to the leads and again, when led to the block, a consummation devoutly wished for by many, and no less by me. One noon, when life became so burdensome that I contemplated abstinence from subsistence so as to end a misery, it was not possible to exist under any more, Allah Inshalla! the door opened, I knew the result! the executioner was at hand! in a few moments, and I'll be free!—

The sensation of the individual at rinsing beneath the iced shower on leaving the close Hammam, is naught in comparison to the bracing of the fresh atmosphere when I first issued upon it. Looking down from the Bridge of Sighs, my sight dazzled by the stinging glare of an Adriatic midday sun, all the more oppressive by the sudden transition from the impenetrable dark of my glowing cell, I beheld a dense mass of upturned faces, fairly packing fthe phza San Marco, to the very brink of the embarkazione, a few minutes more and I stood by the side of the masked executioner, with the point of his broad-billed axe resting upon the block, his hands lapped upon the end of the handle.

Officials read lengthy protocols to the solemn booming of the dolorous bell, a priest fetching up the melancholy rear. As a true believer, I painfully felt it incumbent to decline his good offices, he, poor man, wept to the act until my heart quailed. At a signal, a bandage from behind was placed over my eyes, and all the sweet world was barred from view. I returned the pressure of many an unseen hand, and felt encouraged by a sympathetic murmur pervading among the crowd, for a tyrant was Doge then, at Venice!

Melancholy duties delicately performed are greatly shorn of their painful rigor. The executioner was the last man to clasp my hand and to say a few kindly words, then he tenderly requested me to take one step forward, and then to kneel. I complied more with alacrity than bravadoism, for I had reached the wished for goal, the cynosure of a wished for consummation! Life has no charms when shorn of the charms of life. I was prepared to meet the dread doom, with malice to none and regret for naught. Anything was preferable to the tortures of the broiling, roasting, toasting, griddling, tindering leads!

I knelt. Not in all my life have I experienced a calmness, equalling the instant, when made aware by the whizz that the axe was flashing upward, but to my extreme astonishment, it came down with a thud upon the block to the deafening shout of a sympathizing populace below. "A reprieve! a reprieve!" echoed from end to end of the excited throng, "a reprieve!" Simultaneously with the cry the bandage was removed, once more I was in God's light!

My exultation was but momentary, for a painful regret lest I be returned to the leads made me the only grieved one in that immense joyous gathering.

It was a partial reprieve; my right hand shall redeem the forfeit of my head!

Instantly I stretched my arm upon the block and bade him strike! and as instantly it was off. "Now fly," sternly but kindly whispered the executioner from beneath his mask, "fly quick, or a next command may be once more for the head!"

"Fly and repent," urged the good priest in a whisper, "God is good, but the Doge is vacillating."

This time I followed the good man's behests with a will; no Doge's head rolled those forty steps, faster than I with my bleeding stump bounded down. The dense concourse received me with a deafening shout, and squeezed aside with alacrity to make free my passage to the embarkazione, where a gondola laying alongside, I jumped on board. "Off and away!" I cried, and the craft shot over the breast of the Adriatic's placid ripples!

The gondolier, taking the emergency in at we had a desire to know," after drawing a long breath, which the intensity of the recital, had conferred upon him, remarked one of the audience. "We expected of you to relate the manner by which you accumulated the vast wealth you have."

"The tale was entertaining," interrupted another, "but was not the one we expected and desired."

"Then my friends," good-naturedly put in Yakub Pedir Khan, "I shall have to tell you another, although the tale I told is absolutely necessary to the one to come. By the loss of this hand I gained my fortune, but this circumstance is absolutely inseparable from the sequel, which I will relate to-morrow; that will have reference to

The Phantom Ship
OF SALONIQUE.

"The trip to Constantinople," commenced Yakub Fedir Khan at the next sitting, "un- stances, considerably reassured me. I was his only child, by a wife whom he passionately loved, but who died at giving me birth: Yet my surmises were all ill-grounded, for when he perceived the disaster to my right hand, a crimson flush suddenly flitted hectic flashes to his pallid cheek, and spread with such rapidity that it quickly suffused his entire countenance. His eyes dilated and assumed an unnatural sparkle, appalling to describe much more to behold, as he bolted to an upright sitting posture and wildly exclaimed:

"Allah il Allah! how came I to be worthy of this act of grace!—Inshallah! come to my arms, my boy, you have made me the happiest father alive!"

Great as was his excitement, my perplexity everyway surpassed it. Was it possible to believe my ears, and yet judge my poor old father sane?

"Quick, quick!" cried the old man, after being assured that he was not mistaken as to

WHIR-R-R-R-R IT RUSHED PAST US.

a glance, shot away into mid-stream of the Grand Canal, and taking advantage of a first break, shot around its point, and out of sight.

"Whereto will you now?" demanded the gondolier, for the first time breaking silence.

"Take me to whatever ship is bound for another port," I answered.

"There is but one in the stream, waiting for the land breeze," answered the gondolier "and she is bound for Constantinople."

"Allah il allah!" I exclaimed, "of all the places on earth, it is the port I'd choose; there my father lives. Take me on board, quick!"

In fifteen minutes I was safely cared for under my native flag."

Yakub Fedir Khan stopped.

* * * * *

"But that's not the phase of life of which avoidable incidentals excepted, was accomplished without adventure. But on nearing my boyhood home, my heart misgave me at the grief I had in store for a dear confiding father.

But an incendiary's regret has never yet restored the damage he created; I knocked at my parental door and slinked up-stairs, brow-beaten as a cur, conscious of a misdemeanor. On the way up I learned that my father had been bed-ridden for six weeks. This struck home upon me like remorse at the heels of a murder—my father must have heard of my mishap and had become prostrated by the shock!

The haggardness of the old man as I neared his bedside, absolutely terrified me. To use a common expression, he had fallen away to a cadaverous skeleton, but received me with a warmth which under the circum- the main, "run to the harbor and ascertain if there is a craft which sails for Salonique this day. Before the sun goes down, you must leave for Salonique. Inshalla achbar! that my own loins should have been blessed, to produce a son whose right hand is lopped off! Embrace me son, and help me to bless the Prophet, who makes you instrumental, to confer a blessing on all the world!"

"But father"—I began to expostulate, the old man allowed me no chance to speak, but urged me imperatively to be gone, and to find the desired craft, with the further instructions, that in the event of non-success, to hire one for the purpose, and if none are for charter, to buy one for money.

At the foot of the stairs, I met the captain of the vessel which fetched me from the Adriatic; he came to collect fare, according to agreement, for when in the plight in which he met me at Venice, as I have already mentioned, I had not a coin in my possession.

I told him of my troubles, he listened attentively, and assured me that there was no vessel up for Salonique, but offered his own for charter, and inasmuch as he had come from Venice in ballast, he was ready to sail at any time the breeze should start up. I returned with him to my father's room, who soon struck a bargain for the voyage, and at four o'clock I was passively on board. An old servant, called Caiphar, was detailed to accompany me and with whom father had a long private conference and whom he intrusted with a parchment scroll, securely put up in watertight wrappers. Kissing and blessing me fervently, the old man fell back upon his pillow exhausted, and I never saw him any more. When I returned he had been many days buried.

* * * * * *

A brisk land-breeze, throughout the night, and a prompt sea breeze in the morning, rattled us along at a splendid rate, until nearly noon, when it suddenly slacked off, and in a few moments more, had us as deadly becalmed as at the bottom of a well. The sun was intensely penetrating, and a heavy under swell pitched the helpless craft from side to side, until the spars dipped deep into the glassy surface, which took the appearance of glowing molten lead rather than Mediterranean waters. Everything seemed to partake of the nature of the leads I had lately quitted. All which you touched, fairly singed, and owing to her rolling, not an object afforded more than a momentary shade which, the instant it was cast, the vessel pitched from under it, when the captain, perceiving a small black speck in the far horizon, called my attention to it, which whilst idly gazing upon it, aroused our curiosity to the fact of its perceptibly increasing and in a moment or two more, held out a ship flying before the wind, which delighted us not a little, for it presaged momentary relief to our unpleasant strait.

"By the manner of his looming up," exclaimed the captain, "the fellow is in a hurricane" and immediately gave orders to trim ship for the reception of the coming storm. Scarcely had the order, however, been carried out, when the ship was upon us, and whir-r-r-r it rushed past us [see illustration] and was a speck again ere we could recover from the surprise; for whilst the passing vessel had her sails bellied to bursting and her sheets taut to the snap, the vessel we were on, was lolling and rolling as lazily as if no phenomenon to the contrary had just rushed by, our sails snapping to the naked masts with the discharge of pistols.

But to heighten the horror, was the glance we received of her decks, during the mere instant as she flashed by us. There appeared an impenetrable jam of humanity, who were all wrangling, fighting, shouting, cursing, swearing, shouting, yelling, praying, booting, and killing. Severed heads and limbs were flying in every direction, and streams of blood spurting as from a school of wounded whales; whilst standing upon a heap of slain, his eyes rolling with a ferocity to which nothing likens, most gorgeously attired in silk and gold, with jeweled arms in his sash and a brilliant diamond crescent on his turban, his black beard, silky, wavy, and reaching below his waist, slashing indiscriminately right and left, with his flashing scimitar, whipping heads and limbs off at every pass; stood the giant form of what appeared, the ruling spirit of the desperate sight which at once horrified and charmed us; a spellbound stupor from which our captain was first to recover.

"Allah Achbar!" he exclaimed with heartrending agony, "this was the phantom ship, and we are lost! Woe is me, woe is us all; all which that ship passes is doomed to perish. Our race in life has run!"

Figure to yourself the impression this created among all on board. A desperation set in amongst the crew, it was a hard matter to quell; in a minute everything on board became demoralized, when first a cat's-paw, then a four knot breeze set in to our no little relief, which lasted all night, but perceptibly increased towards morning, and at ten o'clock, compelled us to take in sail; a little later, and we sprang into the jaws of a gale, when snap! first one mast, then another went by, the rudder went next, and the ship spun on crests and dived into troughs with the dexterity of a spinning top in the hands of an Indian juggler.

Caiphar came to my side, and bade me not to lose courage, but follow him to where a boat yet clung to the davits, the rest having been crushed by the falling masts.

"Sit in there with me," said the faithful man, "and at the first fair opportunity, I'll cut her loose, it is our only chance."

Scarcely had I acted upon the advice than the Caiphar freed the boat of her fastenings and almost at the instant, a yell from the ship announced that she had sprung a leak! The vessel at the same time giving a desperate lunge, she plunged stern foremost out of sight drawing our boat into the vortex, and sent us struggling among the wreck into the wild waves.

Although but one arm at command, with the other most excruciatingly painful in consequence of the maimed stump, still blinded as I was by the sudden immersion, I struggled desperately on, and seized hold of the first presentable object, yet, but for a timely grasp upon the clothes at my neck, I should not have retained it long. It was the helping hand of Caiphar which steadied in my great need. He had retained his hold upon the boat at her being drawn into the whirling eddy, but came to the surface with her; she was keel upwards then, still he managed to scramble upon her, and drew me, too, afterwards successfully upon it.

I'll not dwell upon the miseries we endured for the rest of that day and until the middle of the night, when the gale gave way to gentle breezes, and drifting to the current, the moon showed us that we were nearing shore, and to our delight we beheld under the lee of the land, a ship at anchor, and we rapidly drifting towards it.

In vain we hailed with all the strength of our lungs; she appeared completely deserted. We had the satisfaction of grating against her side, and taking advantage of some rope ladders over her sides, swung ourselves upon her decks, when horror! We were on board

THE PHANTOM SHIP OF SALONIQUE!

SEQUEL.

Every yard of the fatal ship was squared and every sail clewed in the most seamanlike manner, but every inch of the decks was littered with heaps of promiscuous slain, from three to ten deep, whilst with his back to the mizzen, stood the fierce man before described, a drawn scimitar in his hand, but pinned at the throat by an iron spike, his point coming out abaft of the mast!

We dreaded stepping upon the ghastly mass, but felt anxious for something to quench our hunger and thirst. To clear a pathway to the cabin, was our only recourse; but to our consternation, everything proved cemented in one. Solid as is grouped casting in bronze! Nothing moving or movable, but our two selves alone! Driven to desperation we bounded over the ghastly pile, touched the fierce man at the mast, he was as a statue of granite or bronze!

Four or five steps led into the cabin, where an exuberance of splendor and wealth surprised us, too dazzling for belief. It was spacious, gorgeous and imposing. A long table in the centre, upheld a sumptuous banquet with every appurtenance of artistic device, and of solid silver, gold and precious stones. We made a bolt for the delicious viands—they were as marble and bronze! Like all on deck, here too, all was solid as if sculptured or cast—nothing detachable but ourselves.

Doors ajar, discovered chambers leading from the cabin, which were filled with treasures appalling to behold, but all adhering to one another, as the dead above and the banquet below. Whole chests of diamonds, sapphire, and other precious stones, which made luminous the surroundings, as by a passing meteor. Everything was of appalling stillness, our own steps even emitted no sound, making silence visible, and the more awful in consequence.

In the midst of this shocking stillness, after a short lapse, a notable disturbance startlingly manifested itself of a sudden; the waters were all at once heard to splash at the ships sides, sailing orders and trampling on the deck became audible; a windlass clicked to anchor chains, loosed sails flapped out to the breeze, and with a significant pitch. lo! the vessel was under way to a gale!

We rushed to the cabin door and peeped in terror over its sill, and behold! with every inch of canvass spread, the ship was impelled to an incredible speed, the decks no more lumbered with dead, and men were properly at their functions, the fierce man freed from the spike, and a dervish at his heels, were coming direct for the cabin and us.

Quickly we resolved to hide ourselves among the treasures, but in passing the banquet, to our delight we perceived everything smoking, and steaming, and loosed from attachment; we snatched at a fowl, and succeeded to hide away, an instant before the dreaded man entered the cabin.

"Woe betide!" we heard the Dervish exclaim. "Woe betide, if you do not mend your ways. More blood cries out aloud for vengeance than would float this ship. There is yet time to repent. Mahomed is great and Allah forgives!"

"Cease your importunities," cried the other sternly, "or you'll drive me to extremes which I shall regret."

"Regret the past," retorted the Dervish, holding his index finger reprovingly towards his companion, repent the present and you'll have no cause for remorse for the future."

"Avaunt!" exclaimed the stern man. "Be your blood upon your own head," saying which he aimed a pass with his scimitar at the head of the Dervish, but which the latter dexterously dodged. Yet the blow alighted on his arm and severed it at the wrist.

"The curse of this deed shall haunt you," exclaimed the Dervish in agony, "at your every step. Until the world ends may you roam, accursed and feared until of my own blood shall spring a redeemer, whom a like cruelty shall deprive of his right hand, and with the remaining one may scatter earth upon you," and rushed up to the deck, the infuriated homicide at his heels.

Quick as it takes me to tell it, all on deck roused itself to the confusion we had witnessed, when the vessel passed us on our second day most. There was hooting, yelling, killing, screaming, clashing of swords and firing of pistols, which, however, slacked with the sun's passing the meridian, and a stillness set in again, as when we came on board.

We ventured diffidently on deck, and judge of our consternation, to find the sails all clewed, the decks piled with dead, the dreadful man with the long beard spiked to the mast by his throat, and the ship at anchor in the harbor of Salonique.

Caiphar understood it all at a glance, he hastily undid the parchment—it confirmed him. He hailed a passing fishing felucca, told me of his plan, and left in the boat for the shore, leaving me on board alone.

Before Caiphar entered the felucca, an idea struck him, the parchment scroll might have some talismanic influence upon the curious predicament we were in, and that it might be detrimental to take it from the ship; he therefore considerately gave it me in charge, which during his absence I made it my business to study well. It dated back a trifle over two hundred years; it named the tall stern man, Malek Adel, and strangely enough, the Dervish bore a name precisely similar to my own. It told the tale exactly as I had seen it enacted that noon, on board the evil ship; but, furthermore, named many significant facts, which, during the formidable melee, in our horrified state, unavoidably escaped us; it confined the ship's passage, during the instant of the sun's passing the meridian, only; and confined her course undeviatingly between the ports of Salonique and Constantinople, but which was to cease when one of the race of him who pronounced the anathema, shall have been cruelly maimed as the Dervish was, and with his left hand strew earth of Salonique upon the whole.

I felt not a little relieved when Caiphar returned alongside, the felucca laden with many sacks of earth. This I sprinkled without hesitation, first on an infant's leg, which vanished as a puffed out candle light. Next, I tried it upon a headless trunk, the result was the same, and in a very little time from its commencement, the deck was freed of all the sickening encumbrance; Malek Adel, erect and spiked to the mizzen, excepted.

The more the decks advanced upon the relief which the earth brought it, the more glowed the glare of the terrific look of the fiend. His eyes rolled with a ferociousness which indicated a savagery of innate malevolence not to be depicted. He seemed conscious of everything going on around him, and Caiphar being a coward, on a par with myself, was but little backward in urging me to pitch earth at him without stint.

Little by little, however, he crumbled to the influence, and the more I beheld him fade away the more courageous I became, until with the collapse of a bursted bladder, a handful of ashes at the step of the mizzen, was all which remained of Malek Adel; but the body of the Dervish was nowhere to be seen; from this I infer, that in the melee he had been consigned to a watery sepulchre.

The influence of the occupation above, had the desired effect upon everything below, where all became individualized as prescribed to natural functions. The viands had crumbled to specks of ashes, the imperishable utensils were all oxidated, rusty, and mildewey, whilst the boxes within the room, had all fallen crumbled to naught, the precious gems scattered over the floors.

Sudden decay and tumbling to ashes was perceptible upon every object, the ship itself inclusive, we hastily filled the sacks with all the treasure available, and quickly decamped from the fading wreck, for scarcely had we embarked upon the felucca, than not a vestige of her was more seen.

IT is amusing to read the stock reports in the daily papers. "A shade lower," "another fall," "heavy break," is the song from day to day. The stolid stupidity of the average San Franciscan is amazing. Cannot any one, but the veriest fool or a chronic gambler, see that Flood & Co. have sucked the orange and thrown the peelings on the sidewalks of Pine and California streets, and that it is over these the fools of fortune are slipping, breaking their limbs and sometimes their necks?

IT is cabled that the British force is cooped up in Cabul, and 15,000 sepoys and hillmen say they will not let them out. The situation is serious, and it makes England's prime minister dizzy to think of it. Cabul will seat Gladstone in Parliament from Midlothian, should there be an election.

CHARLOTTE PATTI has a libel suit against the Pittsburg *Dispatch* for saying she was drunk at a concert. Charlotte *may* have been intoxicated, the mistake is in assigning the cause. She was not "drunk," with champagne, as it were; but only "drunk with delight at her enthusiastic reception.

OREGON desires a population of negroes—she will take 250,000. There is a change in political sentiment since the days of that sturdy old Democrat, Joe Lane—who spelt the name of the Deity with a little g. But, in politics, as in other matters, "it's a long lane which has no turning."

How to marry—get a licence.

[SEE LAST PAGE ILLUSTRATION.]

GUSTAVUS ADOLPHUS,

Seizing a spade from one of the miners, breaks the first earth of the trench around Nuremberg. (*Hist.*)

(*Extract from an unpublished Tragedy of that name.*)

Gustavus Adolphus: Hail Spade!

Entailed by a curse, for both blessing and curse.—

For, necessity, primeval sin's eldest born,

Flung down the spade, humanity to aid.

It constrains the alchemy of passive earth

To yield infant's nutriment, and to prop

With sustenance, manhood's gaining strength.—

In war or peace, the spade must bear the palm;

In life or death, it endless wants, supplies.

The hand that delves, shall garner in the fruit,

Whether crypt for outbreathed mortality,

Or conscientious freedom from ghastly trench.

It is the grand solutionist of all time,—

It has solved the problem of mystic alchemy;

For digging roots is naught but digging gold,—

As aiding war is but suborning peace.—

This, on contriving shift, dawned inventiveness,

And pushed up skill to high meridian.—

In all the world, it is the great creator,

Greatest producer of all greatest needs!—

The spade that delved in

Holy consecrated ground, and firm upheld

The agonies of Him, our Great Redeemer

Now devotedly delves to make that grip

Secure throughout all time.

In our holy cause, each spade is holy,

And emblematic of the sacred Cross.

Defence of Cross by the Cross

Who may question result?

(*Turning to Sappers and Miners.*)

Delve comrades, delve!

And let the piling earth remind of Calvary

The excavations, of planting Cross—all hail!

All dismount--kneel and sing Luther's Hymn.)

(CURTAIN.)

THE ILLUSTRATED WASP.

[See Double-page Cartoon.]

A MIDWINTER NIGHT'S DREAM.

From an unpublished Dramatic Idyl, by MR. SALMI MORSE.

ACT III, SCENE IV.

SCENE.
A FROZEN LAKE, WITH WILD GLACIER SURROUNDINGS.—SNOW KING, DROLLMAN AND SNOWMEN IN GROTESQUE OCCUPATION DISCOVERED.—TO THEM ENTER MINISTER OF CONTENT FROM ABOVE.

Chorus of Snowmen:
       I.
    Rejoice, snow elves, from pole to pole,
    That joy is yours, in lucky dole.
    Where universe dread and forlorn,
    Wallowed, lost, unkempt, unshorn,
    It now exhilerates in haughty scorn
    At an adventitious iceberg born!
       II.
    Crashing, rending, it tumbling leaped,
    In ocean's wide-fenced waters steeped;
    With splashing, hissing, deafening sound,
    Made circles arch to furthest rounds.
    Tidal waves on fierce errand sent
    On earth and sky wild echoes blent!—
       III.
    Monstrous mass, coeval with time!
    Float to dissolve in torrid clime!—
    Revel elf-comrades in your glee!
    A royal snow-offspring now's made free!
    Share his destiny—mount and away!
    For wreck, scourge, shock and dismay!

Snow King. Flaky messengers with portentous haste, are consequentially whirling to level. Let some one interpret their meaning.

Droll. Here is one, King, whose gossamer frame and fern-leaf shapement attracts distinguishment from the myriads that float.

All. Let's see, let's see.

S. King. Simplicity and purity here are evenly blent. This is a forerunner of Heaven-born content.

All. Good, good, good.

S. King. See her come, to make fulsome our auspicious event.

(*Minister of Content descends.*)

All hail, great spirit! our endeavor palls to express the satisfaction, we this moment feel. An iceberg is born to us which without parallel stands, since the first fiat was proclaimed to economize matter. His grossness is antedelurian; a very mastodon of his kind. All the elf squad under my rule are stimulated with a desire to show gratitude.

M. Con. To diffuse contentment is my mission; my object is ever to reconcile to adversity.
    Jove has imposed a task upon me, and I have nominated you co-adjutant.

S. King. Place each snow-man under tribute. All is yours.

M. Con. Your Drollman, which is he?

Droll. Here is he you seek. (*Sings.*)
    I rent me from the Jungfrau brow,
      A baby snowman branch,
    And gathered in my topple down,
      Terrific avalanche.

Chorus of Snowmen:
    The Rhine, the Rhine,
    The beautiful Rhine!
    We melt to water in his lap,
    And he distils it into wine.

Droll. sings:
    The echo of ten thousand hills,
    Applauds my venturous dash,
    And cheers the bold, impetuous leap,
    Long after ceasing to crash.

Chorus of Snowmen:
    The Rhine, the Rhine, etc.

Droll. sings:
    'Tis glorious, 'tis glorious,
    To course such race as mine;
    My father is old Jungfrau hight,
    And I, am father to the Rhine.

Chorus of Snowmen:
    The Rhine, the Rhine, etc.

M. Con. It were folly to detail earthly transpirings to the spirit world, where actions are registered as accomplished, at inception.
    Assist me to end the tribulations of that bereaved mother whose crazed ravings add hideousness to the night's disorganization.

All. We will, we will, we will.

M. Con. Some one, then, stop at once this snow racket, while some others drift your wild snowfall, so that the benighted wayfarer, in the midnight desolation, and wildness of the moor, may not halt undecided, whether to advance or not. May he struggle on to where that poor woman roams in worse indecision than he. There impede him so, that he may stumble upon her whereabouts. She is his wife, and he her husband, for two winters supposed to be lost.

Droll. That will I. (*Sings.*)
    I'll bob at his horse,
      Both before and behind,
    And bring him to halt,
      So the woman he'll find.

Chorus of Snowmen:
    We'll bob at his horse,
      Both before and behind,
    And break through the drift,
      So the woman he'll find.

M. Con. To your task, good Snow-men, whilst the King and I plan further shapement to the destiny of these mortals.

(*Exit Minister Content and Snow King.*)

Droll. (*Sings.*)
    The snowman's father of the stream,
    That feeds both earth and sea,
    'Tis he sustains all universe,
    In present, past, eternity.

Chorus of Snowmen:
    A snowman is a wondrous elf,
    He roams through space, on scudding clouds,
    He thrones on highest mountain peak,
    And drapes them in his fleecy shrouds.

Droll. Sings:
    He curbs volcano's fiery wrath,
    By ice-grip throttle near its cone,
    And poises on its snowy palm
    The red-hot lava, molten stone.

Chorus of Snowmen:
    A snowman is a wondrous elf, etc.

THE nose is to man what the horn is to the quadruped. Individuals, snubbing their noses in derision, often gore more effectively than bulls with their horns. The vulgar make up for their lack of rhetoric by the snubbing of their noses. Whisky bloats, by their noses belong to the family Rye-nose-rose.

THE finance report of the Author's Carnival, leads us to believe that there was a general misapprehension of the purpose for which it was undertaken. The list of varied expenditures and their amounts, show that all the literary larceny and dramatic drudgery was in the interest of our suffering retail trade and the newspapers. "Charity was only a curtain that hid the design from sight."

THE police have their periodical spasm of virtue. It occurs with the accession of every new chief to office. Crowley is the man who is giving the faro-boys a lively lay-out at present, and proposes to shut up all the "hogging" games in town in favor of the "square" dealers. From a policeman's standpoint, the game is not so much considered as the people who play it.

SEDATE—in the almanac.

WINTER'S NIGHT'S DREAM
PAGE 359

BEYOND THE MOON!
A CHRISTMAS LIE.
NOT BY
JULES VERNE.

The edict was forth! The suitor who will tell the most impossible tale, shall obtain the coveted hand of the Princess Guldhir. Abdul Hillil told the one which follows, and won the prize.

Among the many commodities on board my vessel, were some cases of nitro-glycerine on freight, for which there appeared no claimant. Shipping was dull in port, freight scarce; everything had assumed the appearance of a lengthened stay, and hearing of good sport near the Cashmere lakes of the Himalayas, I shouldered my gun and prepared myself for a good time.

There are many present, who have made trips to the Himalayas, and whom its uninteresting detail would but annoy. Suffice it to say, I reached a point in the ascent, where elephants were no more available for aid; but where every crag was alive with every possible species of game for sport, indigenous to the higher latitudes.

The circumstance suggested no choice of action, but to secure my animals near some running stream, to lay before them an ample supply of provender, and to follow the bent of my enterprise on foot.

As fortune would have it, near a gurgling spring, spinning its silvery threads from out an aperture in the rock, stood a clump of young banyan trees in stately array. I snatched at the opportunity and tethered the elephants there, for the manifold reason of there being ready feed, drink, and shade, taking the double precaution of hobbling the beasts so they might not escape, and of tying them far enough apart to keep them out of mischief.

That done, I vigorously strapped to, and for two entire days and nights, gathered grasses, of which I piled a complete stack before each, then started with alacrity in search of adventure.

Not Nimrod of old, with all the world's forests replete with unscared game, had chances equalling mine. At each lifting of the gun, it was a matter of choice with me, whether I slayed a rabbit, a lion, an eagle, a quail or rhinoceros, or one of hundreds of other species, for which lowly man has no name yet. They were mixed and huddled together, thicker than tame flocks in low valleys, but so excessively indiscriminate and docile, that the fact appalled.

Here no human foot ever trod, no human cruelty ever thinned the over abundance.

It was the eighth day out, when I began to feel so tired and surfeited with the sport, that I concluded to retrace my way to the ship, when a unicorn, white as the snowy crest it pastured on, and of proportions, which exemplified symmetry personified hove in sight. I became ambitious to maim and capture it, and to fetch it away alive.

I brought my gun forward, which for convenience, I carried pendent at my back to a strong breast strap over my chest, and because the unicorn was beyond shooting range, I commenced the task of clambering after him. Heedless of consequences, as all keen sportsmen are, I recklessly climbed and bounded from eminence to eminence, and from crag to crag, until I was brought to a sudden halt, by an awkward formation of rock which put a check to all possible advance. I was completely brought to, by an abrupt ending over an abyss, where distant roar announced a tremendous rush of water beneath, but whose intense profundity defied the penetration of sight.

Annoyed at my disappointment, and night coming on apace, I concluded to retrace and make camp.

I supped with a keen appetite, near by a delicious streamlet, and slept soundly until the sun was high the next day.

Having no affairs requiring alacrity, I lazily lolled among the luxurious grasses around me, when a pendant line attracted my vision, with its lowest end tangled into an inextricable mass. It was of nondescript color, and had the appearance of a vertical cobweb thread, only that it was so excessively fine, that a human hair in comparison was a ship's cable. I leisurely walked towards it, and agreeable to the destructive instinct of perverted nature, at once set to, to break it; but to my consternation it resisted the utmost efforts of every available application, and even defied my knees, hands, teeth, and knife, as stubbornly as an anchor chain would.

A new idea possessed me now, to unhitch it from its belaying point, and have it to take home with me as a curiosity. I first began to pull at it, by fitting jerks for so slight a thread, the force of the application increasing to the exigence of its tenaciousness, but it defiantly resisted all. I have it, I thought! I would fire it in two with my gun! Out of twenty bullets, more than half split in two by the contact, the rest missed.

Now, I, who have overcome obstacles but to the lot of very few, shall I be baffled by so trivial a thing as a thread, not the hundredth part the thickness of a hair? No! I became ashamed of my inability, and at once formed a resolution to suspend my whole weight on it, and may be thereby break it down. It defied my most persistent efforts.

I never felt so humiliated in my life. I felt smaller than a grease spot which everybody despises. Had I been a naturalist, with predilection for scientific discoveries, its tenacious resistance might have been grateful to my enthusiasm, but no; I am a sailor, brusque, rude, impetuous and matter of fact, I felt baffled by such an insignificance, that a fly pushing against ought to sunder. I pondered awhile, then came to the resolve, that if the mountain refuses to come to Mahomet, Mahomet must go to the mountain, and if my neck breaks in the attempt, I'll go up it.

The wild resolution and the hair brained effort were put into execution as quick as the thought was hatched, and up, up, up, I went, as fast as a hand over hand movement would let me, until night set in, and fatigue suggested repose. My experience upon the handling of ropes, made it an easy task to bend loops around hands and feet, and thus apparently secured against accidental falling, I soon fell asleep.

I awoke invigorated the next morning, freed my limbs from the loops, and set afresh upon the task before me, and thus continued on for several days until I entered upon regions where day and night know no partition. The surprising wonders which enraptured my astonished senses, can neither be imagined nor described. I passed through regions of conflicting currents whose fierce blasts ripped my clothes into shreds, until naught but my gun was remaining upon me, which, owing to its being slung on by a strong strap, defied the blasts.

Blank as looks the atmosphere between earth and space, just so much to the contrary is it peopled with a mass of varied creation, which have no comparison below, and consequently have no classification. Every thing there appears winged, but absolutely devoid of nether limbs, thereby emphatically asserting the fact, that they exist upon the wing only, and judging by the general harmony prevailing there, subsistence is derived from atmospheric inhalation solely.

This is no far fetched hyperbole, but grounded upon practical demonstration. The gnawing crave I had for something to eat, gradually subsided when entering upon the gifted atmospheric belt, and had entirely deserted me, when I was fairly in the midst of it. [See "*A Landscape on the Moon.*"]

On the eighth day out, measuring time by space, I passed the moon, whose horrid aspect fearfully appalled me. A boundless continent was floating in mid air, and consisted of a frowning jumble of fantastic peaks, whose rayless light conjured reflecting shadows in such unnatural contrast to its pallid white, that its horrid grandeur inspired a tremor upon me which came with, in an ace of shattering my consciousness. It appeared to be full of profound chasms and horridly yawning craters, and inspired a terror to which nothing likens. But there were myriads of other such bleak and inhospitable bodies which owe perception by their sharp ridges, jagged points, and immeasurably harassing aspect. It conveyed the impression to me of floating amidst a continental tombstone family of blasted and bleak moonlit sepulchre!

I frequently passed through fields, which below are known by the term of flying scud, but in the upper regions represent the iceberg floats of the atmospheric Arctic, gracefully steering clear of each other at casual contact, and delicately crumbling, when clashing with the thread I swung to.

At the passing of one of these hurrying fields, a crowning delight overtook me. I beheld a boundless body floating upon the impenetrable darkness overhead, and only distinguishable by a lurid, rayless reflection upon the blank spaces yet higher up, for my sense of touch indicated that my delicate support had attachment there, and that I was near the end of my difficult toil. The darkness now became perceptible to touch; it felt to the grasp like foam in a washbowl, and although of such intense black to which there is no comparison, still objects were visible with appalling distinctiveness, entirely outstripping the more extravagant visionary penetrativeness below.

Huge, formless, but appalling masses, with variable speed, plodded by a dull and clumsy gait, in every direction, palpably manifesting in every part of their monstrous shapelessness, a recognition of my daring intrusiveness, and by voices of tangible thunder conversed by a visible oratory, portentously significant, undergoing constant transformation as a sandy desert during a sirocco blast.

Passing the belt of these awful wonders, my goal was reached. A projecting peninsula, reaching out from the main mass, held the belaying end of my perilous causeway. A dexterous but risky jump, and I stood upon it!

It felt solid as terra firma, but was all ablaze! One uninterrupted, dancing, shooting, licking, crackling, lurid, vehement flame! To liken its intensity to the flame of usage, would be to compare a mammoth cavern to a needle's eye.

But I was too much pleased at my journey's end, and too tired for observation at that moment. My uppermost desire was to stretch out for rest and sleep. The constant and excessive strain upon my limbs for so many consecutive days, called aloud for relaxation. But I looked in vain for a propitious spot, whereon to refresh my strained and aching limbs, for look where I would, all was blaze, glow, scorch, swelter, and singe. The only remedy which suggested itself, was to clear a place to stretch my aching bones upon, and fagged as I was, I set about it with wonderful alacrity, and shortly upon was soundly asleep.

I have no conception what length of time I slept, but I waked with a craving hunger gnawing upon my susceptibilities, which almost frenzied me. A long, dark, shadowy form, which the universal combustion seemed in no manner to affect, now hove in sight, stamping a trail of footprints in its course. I drew sight upon my gun, paff! The beast rolled over upon the flame with the splash of the Himalaya range into the ocean pitched. A salamander had fallen! I feasted.—

The extremities of the beast reached beyond ordinary occular range, but it steaded me mightily as a pathway to my explorations. I walked on its length for many a day, slept upon it and fed from it at the same time. A few days' investigation convinced me of many facts. I could distinguish with indubitable correctness, mountains, valleys, forests, streams, and seas, but everything of a nature of inscrutable flame, glow and heat, but so utterly void of a solitary redeeming point, that I abruptly concluded to abandon the freaky sphere and to return. Nearing my place of starting, to my great dismay, I discovered a dangerous chafe in the line, the effect of strain and friction near to the belaying end, which I carefully spliced, and at once commenced a dash for the downward course.

I slid smoothly and rapidly downward with every prospect of an uninterrupted and rapid voyage, when paff! raff! whir-r-r-r! the thread snapped on the strain, and away I whirled head over heels, until a granite peak received me, up to my neck imbedded in a mineral grip!

In the fearful downward whirl, my gun and I had parted, two days later it too came down, and imbedded to the rule of myself, its lesser weight procrastinating its transit.

At this stage of the relation, the orator paused.

"How came you clear of the granite grip?" exclaimed the Caliph, in the hope of perplexing Abdul Hillil-in the end.

"Easy enough," coolly interposed the other, "*I fetched me a case of the unclaimed nitro-glycerine, and blew myself and my gun clear!*"

BUZZINGS.

"BULL BUTTER," fraudulently conveyed into trade, is playing the mischief with the dairymen in New York. It was considered a fat thing at one time, especially in San Francisco, where Paraff and Vernon Seaman sold oleomargerine stock on a margin. Seaman

A LANDSCAPE ON THE MOON.

has gone East. Paraff went to Chile where he tried to transmute copper into gold as he said he had suet into butter. Chilenos wouldn't have it, and now he is sighing an exile in Valdivia.

GEORGE AUGUSTUS SALA, a good writer, but a better epicure, is doing Hamerica for the *London Telegraph,* and will take in San Francisco among other places. Some say he comes only as a correspondent; others, who know him, will say he is an invalid and travels to get rid of his gout. Be this as it may. There is no doubt he will get rid of a great deal of Anglo-Saxon bile regarding this "blarsted country."

THE new Postal order is working well we are told; that is, green post office clerks and ignorant route agents are learning geography by the extra trouble imposed upon correspondents in addressing their letters. The postal pap-suckers, in fact, now make the public do most of their work and pay them besides. The old hands met the public half way at least on this proposition.

ABOUT this time the pupils of the different Public Schools convert themselves into nuisances to their friends and the public generally, by soliciting contributions to make a Christmas present to "dear teacher." The young ladies and gentlemen of the ferule ought to discountenance this practice. Times are too hard—too hard. Besides there is an ordinance of the Board of Education against it. Scholars bearing gifts lead to favoritism, and to injurious comparisons between the poor boy or girl and the one whose parents are well to do.

SEVERAL purple noses grew pale at the news that the brandy crop had failed in France, and did not recover color till they heard Barry had received a fresh consignment from Nagles. It is said to be as good as the stocks "in the great houses lining the Charenty."

"GAS" seems to be a prominent feature in our social economy. If it ceases to flow temporarily at the various balls and Sand-lot, we find it claiming recognition by bursting up through the streets. Converting the remark of a celebrated his personage, concerning disciples, to a mean use, we may say of the agitators, that "if they hold their peace, the very stones seem to cry out."

FORTUNE hunting is on the rampage again. This time it is the Springer family who look to have 80,000,000 dollars divided among them, the accumulated riches of a dead and gone progenitor, a wealthy Swede who owned 18,000 acres in New Netherlands. The Springer's have apparently a tough job to straighten out the till; but they are at work on it, and "Hope springs eternal in the human breast."

KEARNEY has left us for six weeks. *Laus Deo.* But we feel sorry for the East, particularly for Washington.

For Elegant Suits, Men's and Boys', go to PALMER'S 726 Market St

364   THE ILLUSTRATED WASP.

An Entirely New Invention.
WHEELER & WILSON'S
New Number 8
Straight Needle
SEWING MACHINE.

Not the Old Machine Improved.   *The work passed from the Operator*

This machine will do a greater variety of work than any other in the market.

It is the most simple and durable, and will give the operator the least trouble to work it.

Don't buy a sewing machine until you have seen it. Send for descriptive price list.

WHEELER & WILSON, Manufacturing Co.,
20 GEARY STREET, SAN FRANCISCO.

IT STANDS AT THE HEAD!
"DOMESTIC"
SEWING MACHINE,
SAVES MUSCLE, HEALTH, TIME, TEMPER.

The Lightest Running Lock-Stich Sewing Machine in the Market.

It is PERFECT in every feature, and COMPLETE in all its details. It embodies all of the MODERN Improvements that are of PROVED VALUE.

J. W. EVANS, 29 Post Street,
Mechanics' Institute Building.

GLOVE BUYERS
Buckskin, - $6.00 per Dozen and upwards.
Goatskin, - - 4.00 "   "   "   "

WILLIAM SHIRES, Manufacturer,
516 PINE STREET.
Orders or Correspondence solicited.

BARNEY CURRAN
has opened and fitted up in a first class style a store No. 6 Clara Lane, corner of Berry Place. The best Wines, Liquors and Cigars constantly on hand. A good warm luncheon served at noon time. Mr. Curran will be glad to see his old patrons. Give him a call,

Ladies, Take Notice!
Having bought at Sheriff's Sale the entire stock of Millinary goods of Miss Wood, No. 8 Kearny street, we now offer elegant hats and bonnets at less than the cost of the material; also a new invoice of French kid button boots at $2.50 a pair. Chicago Auction House, 134 Sixth street.

Philadelphia Brewery.
—Philadelphia Brewery has sold during the year 1878 43,107 barrels of beer, being twice as much as the next two leading breweries in this city (See Official Report, U. S. Internal Revenue January, 1879.) The beer from this Brewery has a Pacific Coast renown, unequaled by any other upon the Pacific Coast. *

SNOW & CO.
(Late Snow & May.)

Importers and Dealers in works of Art. Novelties in picture frames a specialty. All the new engravings and photogravures as soon as published. 20 POST ST., S. F.

United Co-Operative Boot and Shoe Store,
605 Kearney street, between Sacramento and Commercial. A full line of Ladies, Gents, Misses, and Boys' work, of our own manufacture kept on hand. Buy here and encourage White Labor. Send for our price list.

THE CHEAPEST PLACE TO BUY OR RENT
PIANOS
IS AT
B. CURTAZ, 20 O'Farrell St.

THE RIGHT PLACE IS THE
IMPERIAL,
724 1-2 MARKET STREET.
FOR THE
VERY BEST PICTURES OF ALL KINDS
Best Floating Cabinets, per doz. $5.00.
Best Floating Cards, per doz. $2.50.

OSBORN & ALEXANDER
628 Market St., opp. Palace.

HARDWARE AND Mechanics' Tools

ELITE Scroll Saw only $4.50. VELOCIPEDE Scroll Saws $15.00 and $17.50, LESTER Saw combining scroll and circular and turning Lathe, $12.00.

TOY CANNONS, $1.00
Parlor Air Guns and Pistols, all styles.
POCKET KNIVES, Fine Assortment.

D. Callaghan & Co.
MANUFACTURERS OF
DONNOLLY'S
Premium Yeast Powder
CALLAGHAN'S
CREAM TARTAR, SODA AND SALERATUS
COFFEE AND SPICES
119 and 121 FRONT ST., S. F.

Smoke the sweetest and best flavored
OLD JUDGE

Smoke the Gentleman's Tobacco
OLD JUDGE

Smoke the best in the World
OLD JUDGE

THE ILLUSTRATED WASP. 365

THE WORLD RENOWNED
Bohemian Ladies Orchestra
—AT—
"THE FOUNTAIN"
RESTAURANT, OYSTER AND REFRESHMENT SALOON,
ILLUMINATED WITH ELECTRIC LIGHT,
S. E. Corner Kearny and Sutter Streets,
SAN FRANCISCO.
Ladies Entrance Elevator on Kearny Street and Ver Mehr Places.
☞ Daily Lunch and Dinners served at any time, up to 8 P. M

WM. HESSE, Jr., Proprietor.

Opera, Field,   Marine Glasses.

The BEST and CHEAPEST place in the city to buy SPECTACLES, EYE-GLASSES, OPERA, FIELD and MARINE GLASSES, etc., with a guarantee to suit, is at
BERTELING & WATRY,
Scientific Opticians 427 Kearny Street, S. F.

WESTERFELD & PAGE'S
BAKERY & RESTAURANT,
745 Market Street, bet. Third and Fourth, opp. Dupont, San Francisco.
☞ OPEN TO 12 O'CLOCK P. M.
Lunch and Dinners for Weddings, etc., supplied in the best style to private residences at short notice.
☞ All kinds of bread and confectionery on hand or made to order and delivered to any part of the city.

SEWER GAS STOPPED AT LAST.
W. E. LANE'S
Pat. Triplet Sewer Trap.
Shuts out all sewer gas at the sidewalk and sends fresh air up into all the pipes and sewers in your House instead.

Call and see the Triplet Sewer Trap in use in the sewer at W. E. Lane's, The Plumber and Sanitary Engineer, No. 505 Kearny Street, near California, or send for circulars. Sanitary Plumbing Sewerage and ventilating Houses, etc., a specialty.

The best CIGARETTES in the World
OLD JUDGE

The TIVOLI GARDENS
Eddy Street, bet. Market and Mason.
KREELING BROS..............Proprietors
Rendezvous of the Elite, and the only Garden of its kind in America.

H. M. S. PINAFORE
—AND—
Trial by Jury.
MUSIC BY
THE GRAND TIVOLI ORCHESTRA,
Under the Leadership of MR. J. M. NAVONI, lately from New York.

SAINT ANN'S REST.
SCHMIDT & BUTLER, Proprietors.
Every Evening, until further notice, will be produced at this popular place of amusement
☞ THE GREAT EVENT OF THE CENTURY! ☜
A GREAT PHENOMENON,
The Egyptian Mystery!
This Entertainment is
SCIENTIFIC,
ARTISTIC,
ASTOUNDING and
SENSATIONAL.
Doors open at 7 o'clock.

OH, AH!
MULLER
The Leading Optician,
135 MONTGOMERY ST.,
Near Bush, opposite the Occidental Hotel.
SPECTACLES.—Their adaptation to the various conditions of sight has been my specialty for
30 YEARS!
Directions and Price Lists mailed free. Orders by all or Express promptly attended to.
☞ PRICES REDUCED! ☜
C. MULLER, Optician,
135 MONTGOMERY, near Bush.
Established in San Francisco, 1863.

FALKENSTEIN & CO. 300 Battery Street,
OLD JUDGE

VIENNA
Concert Gardens
Cor. Sutter and Stockton Sts.
(Formerly the TIVOLI.)
THE GREAT FAMILY RESORT.
THE CELEBRATED
VIENNA
Ladies' Orchestra
Has been engaged permanently for
INSTRUMENTAL and VOCAL CONCERTS,
Nightly Performance of the well known Xylophone and Cornet Soloist, MR. WILLIAM FORNER.
Commencing every Evening at 8 o'clock.
MATINEE CONCERT, every Sunday 3 P. M. Sharp
☞ FAMILY LUNCH, FROM 11 A. M. DAILY.
The enlarged Hall and Gardens have been thoroughly renovated, beautified, and fitted up as a FIRST CLASS FAMILY RESORT.   RIECK & CO., Proprietors.

TATUM & BOWEN,
329 Market and 3 Fremont Streets,
San Francisco.

Patented Dec 17, 1878, by R. Hoe & Co.
SOLE AGENTS FOR
The following Machinery, much of which is ENTIRELY DIFFERENT from any other, and therefore should be seen by parties before purchasing.
☞ R. Hoe & Co's World Renowned Printing and Lithograph Presses. (The Chronicle Presses, recently furnished, are the finest in the world.)
R. Hoe & Co's Ventilating Chisel-Tooth and Shop Saws.
Stearns Manufacturing Co's Pacific Saw Mill Machinery. (The heaviest and most ingenious ever made.) Automatic Out-off Saw Mill Engines. Corliss and Ball Patent Valve Engines and Boilers. Best English Babbit. Boiler Scale Eradicator. Leather and Gum Belting.

Send for Catalogue.

MRS. M. WAGNER,
FASHIONABLE
DRESS AND CLOAK MAKER
1024½ Larkin St. Near Sutter,
SAN FRANCISCO.

Sole Agents for the Pacific Coast for
OLD JUDGE

MUSIC BOXES
....FOR....
WEDDING AND BIRTHDAY PRESENTS,

M. J. PAILLARD & CO.
Manufacturers and Importers,

31 POST STREET.
A. J. JUILLERAT,
Sole Agent for the Pacific Coast.
Factory, St. Croix, Switzerland. Music Boxes thoroughly Repaired.

CHARLES F. HERTWECK,
UPHOLSTERER.
Drapery made and Repaired.
902 LARKIN ST., bet. Post and Geary.

CHARLES F HERTWECK,
Practical Teacher on the ZITHER.
Music for Concerts, Serenades, Parties, etc., furnished at reasonable rates.

P. LIESENFELD
BILLIARD, POOL and BAGATELLE TABLES. Sole Agent Phelan & Collender's New Improved Patent Cushions, Billiard Goods, etc. No 585 MARKET STREET, S. F.

$25 to $5000 Judiciously invested in Wall St. lays the foundation for fortunes every week, and pays immense profits by the New Capitalization System of reporting in Stocks. Full explanation on application to ADAMS, BROWN & CO., Bankers, 18 Broad St., N. Y.

ONCE USED!
Always Used!

EMIL FRESE'S HAMBURG TEA is the best family medicine, and will be found on trial to be the most easy, natural and comfortable aperient obtainable.

EMIL FRESE'S HAMBURG TEA will act gently on the bowels, remove wind, cure heartburn, sour stomach and dizziness and promote a healthy secretion of bile.

EMIL FRESE'S HAMBURG TEA is the most effectual remedy for headache, giddiness, nervous depression, palpitation of the heart, lassitude and general debility.

EMIL FRESE'S HAMBURG TEA gives speedy and durable relief in bilious and liver complaints, weak digestion, shivering, spasms, low spirits and irritability.

EMIL FRESE'S HAMBURG TEA is invaluable as a remedy for the piles. It has been tried for many years and has given great satisfaction. If you are afflicted try it.

EMIL FRESE'S HAMBURG TEA has an established reputation as an efficacious remedy for sudden and severe colds coughs, fevers and ague asthma and phthisis.

EMIL FRESE'S HAMBURG TEA cures chronic, nervous and sick headache, nervous depression, drowsiness, nausea, vomiting, pimples on the face and freckles.

EMIL FRESE'S HAMBURG TEA is a gentle laxative and tonic; improves the appetite, cures dyspepsia, and counteracts the effect of malarious poison.

EMIL FRESE'S HAMBURG TEA cures constipation, diarrhœa and dysentery is certain in results, and corrects all disturbances of the stomach and bowels.

EMIL FRESE'S HAMBURG TEA is the best medicine for children. As a spring remedy nothing comes near to it. Everybody should use it at the change of seasons.

For Sale by every DRUGGIST, GROCER, and COUNTRY MERCHANT, on the Pacific Coast.

PRICE 25 CENTS PER PACKAGE.

NICOLL, THE TAILOR!
Branch of New York.

Being our own Importers, we are able to guarantee and give the REAL article at such prices as defy competition. We sell goods to suit the Banker, Merchant and Clerk. Gentlemen, before calling elsewhere will do well to call and

INSPECT MY IMMENSE STOCK!
DO NOT FAIL TO SEE
THE ELECTRIC LIGHT!

Call and see the ELECTRIC LIGHT at NICOLL'S by which colors and quality may be seen as clear at NIGHT as at NOONDAY

Pants, from - - $5.00	Black Doeskin
Suits. from - - -$20.00	Pant, from - - $8.00
Overcoats, from - $20.00	White Vests, from $3.00
Dress Coats, from $20.00	Fancy Vests, from $6.00

Genuine 6 x Beaver Suits, $55.00.

Samples, with Instructions for Self-Measurement, Sent Free.

ONLY WHITE LABOR employed, and none but EXPERIENCED and FIRST-CLASS Cutters. A small stock of Uncalled-for Goods at Immense Reductions.
SALE PRICES—Pants from $6; Suits from $12; Overcoats from $10; Vests from $2; Coats from $7.
The trade and Public supplied with Cloth and Trimmings at Wholesale Prices. Any length cu., and all kinds of stock kept on hand.

THE FINEST STOCK OF WOOLENS IN THE WORLD.
NICOLL, THE TAILOR'S, Grand Tailoring Emporium
727 MARKET STREET.

H. T. HELMBOLD'S
COMPOUND
FLUID EXTRACT
BUCHU,
PHARMACEUTICAL

A Specific Remedy for all
DISEASES
—OF THE—
Bladder and Kidneys

For Debility, Loss of Memory, Indisposition to Exertion or Business, Shortness of Breath, Troubled with Thoughts of Disease, Dimness of Vision, Pain in the Back, Chest, and Head, Rush of Blood to the Head, Pale Countenance, and Dry Skin.
If these symptoms are allowed to go on, very frequently Epileptic Fits and Consumption follow. When the constitution becomes affected it requires the aid of an invigorating medicine to strengthen and tone up the system—which

"Helmbold's Buchu"
DOES IN EVERY CASE.

HELMBOLD'S BUCHU
IS UNEQUALED!

By any remedy known. It is prescribed by the most eminent physicians all over the world, in

Rheumatism, Gen'l Debility, Spinal Diseases, Spermatorrhœa, Kidney Diseases, Sciatica, Neuralgia, Liver Compl't, Deafness, Nervousness, Nervous Debility Decline, Dyspepsia, Epilepsy, Lumbago, Indigestion, Head Troubles, Catarrh, Constipation, Paralysis, Nerv's Compl't, Aches and Pains, Gen'l Ill-Health, Female Comp'ts

Headache, Pain in the Shoulders, Cough, Dizziness, Sour Stomach, Eruptions, Bad Taste in the Mouth, Palpitation of the heart Pain in the region of the Kidneys, and a thousand other painful symptoms, are the offsprings of Dyspepsia.

HELMBOLD'S BUCHU
INVIGORATES THE STOMACH.

And stimulates the torpid Liver, Bowels, and Kidneys to healthy action, in cleansing the blood of all impurities, and imparting new life and vigor to the whole system.
A single trial will be quite sufficient to convince the most hesitating of its valuable remedial qualities.

Price $1.00 Per Bottle,
or Six Bottles for $5.00.

livered to any address free from observation
"Patients" may consult by letter, receiving the same attention as by calling, by answering the following question:
1 Give your name and post-office address, county and State, and your nearest express office
2 Your age and sex?
3 Occupation?
4 Married or single!
5 Height, weight, now and in health!
6 How long have you been sick?
7 Your complexion, color of hair and eyes?
8 Have you a stooping or erect gait?
9 Relate without reservation all you know about your case Enclose one dollar as consultation fee. Your letter will then receive our attention, and we will give you the nature of your disease and our candid opinion concerning a cure.
Competent Physicians attend to correspondents Al letters addressed to Dispensatory, 1517 Filbert street, Philadelphia, Pa.

H. T. HELMBOLD.
Druggist and Chemist, Philadelphia, Pa.

SOLD EVERYWHERE.

Henry Ahrens. Henry Tietjen. Th. v. Borstel.
CHICAGO BREWERY,
1420--1434 Pine St., near Polk.
Henry Ahrens & Co.
Proprietors.

DRY NO. I RUSTIC.
—SOLD AT—
F. KORBEL & BROS.
Corner Bryant and Fifth Streets.

AUGUST WOLFF,
BOOK BINDER,
310 POST ST., bet. Stockton and Powell.

Sample Cards, Folios, etc., made to order. Music Books bound in 36 hours' notice. Orders for binding from the country will be filled with neatness and dispatch.

PATENT COVERS
For Filing the WASP.

Can be obtained at the office at 50 cents a piece.

AGENTS! READ THIS!

We will pay Agents a Salary of $100 per month and expenses, or allow a large commission, to sell our new and wonderful inventions. We mean what we say. Sample free. Address SHERMAN & CO., Marshall, Mich.

Corns, Bunions, Ingrowing

Nails, Freckles, Warts, Moles, effectually cured by the celebrated Chiropodists,

FEISTEL & GERARD, from Paris,

536 Market Street, opp. Fourth. Parlors 2 and 3, up stairs.

ORDERS taken at the WASP'S Business Office, 602 California St.

CPSIA information can be obtained
at www.ICGtesting.com
Printed in the USA
BVHW061507041218
534743BV00020B/1358/P